MAKE YOUR OWN ADVENTURE

Bluebelle and the
RUNAWAY BALLOON

Illustrations by Colin Petty
Written by Stewart Cowley

DERRYDALE BOOKS
NEW YORK

Published 1985 by
Derrydale Books
Distributed by
Crown Publishers, Inc.

Produced for Derrydale Books by
Victoria House Publishing Ltd.,
4/5 Lower Borough Walls,
Bath BA1 1QR, England.

Copyright © 1985 Victoria House
Publishing Ltd.

Printed in Belgium.

THE ADVENTURE

When Bluebelle is whisked away in Professor Clatterpop's brightly colored balloon, an exciting chase for her friends, the Valley Folk, begins.
No one knows how or where it will end. As you read the story, you will discover that there are decisions to be made — look for the signposts on the pages. Often there will be two choices with a different page number beside each one. When you have decided what Bluebelle and the Valley Folk should do, turn to the page number shown, and discover where you have led them! If you're not given a choice, the signposts will show you the way.
Have a good adventure, and remember, the choice is yours!

It was a bright but windy day as Bluebelle wandered through the woods, admiring the wild flowers. Something large and brightly colored suddenly caught her eye through the trees.

"My!" she gasped. "It's Professor Clatterpop's balloon. I wonder what it's doing here." She stepped into the clearing where the balloon swayed gently in the breeze. It was tied down by a big,

heavy rope. Bluebelle couldn't resist taking a closer look.

"It's beautiful," she murmured, standing on tiptoe and peeking into the basket. "I'm sure the Professor won't mind if I sit inside." There were cushions to sit on and a big lever to pull. "How nice it would be," she thought, "to go up just a little way." But she knew she really ought to wait for the Professor.

SHE WAITS 8

SHE PULLS THE LEVER 12

7

Bluebelle threw two big, heavy sandbags out of the basket so she could sit comfortably. The balloon bobbed and swayed a little more in the breeze, but Bluebelle didn't notice. Soon the gentle rocking of the basket put her to sleep.

The wind started to rise, and the balloon tugged and pulled and strained at its rope, until with a sharp crack it snapped. Free at last, the balloon rose up through the trees.

The jolt woke Bluebelle up, but the forest lay far beneath her. It made her dizzy to look. "Oh, how will I get down?" she cried. At that

moment the basket bumped into a big, white, fluffy cloud.

Bluebelle looked up and to her amazement saw that a large and very untidy nest sat on the highest point of the clouds.

"Maybe whoever lives there could help me," she thought. "Or should I try the lever? If I pull it hard enough, perhaps the balloon will go down!"

SHE CLIMBS OUT — 10

SHE PULLS THE LEVER — 12

Bluebelle was about to step onto the cloud when a voice cried out, "Stop! Don't get out, you'll fall right through!" and a very strange, scruffy looking bird tumbled out of the nest in a flurry of feathers. "Pardon me for shouting," said the bird—who was called Cloud Cuckoo. "You see, I'm used to walking on clouds and you're not. Are you . . . er . . . lost?"

"Yes," said Bluebelle, and she told Cloud Cuckoo about her adventures. Cloud Cuckoo thought for a moment.

"I could whistle up a wind to blow you home if you like."

"Oh, yes please!" cried Bluebelle excitedly.

Cloud Cuckoo looked doubtful. "The only thing is, I'm not sure if I can remember the right tune. Perhaps I should try to find the Professor instead. What do you think?"

LOOK FOR THE PROFESSOR 14

WHISTLE UP A WIND 20

11

The balloon suddenly shot upwards. Bluebelle held on tightly. Far below her friends from Meadowfree were enjoying a picnic. She shouted down to them, but she was too far away, and no one heard her.

"I must get them to look up," she thought, and picking up a cushion, she hurled it over the side.

Just then she passed above a fluffy cloud with a very strange nest on top of it. Suddenly, a large, scruffy bird emerged from the nest —and flew straight into the cushion!

"Oof!" went the bird, whose name was Cloud Cuckoo, falling back in a heap onto the cloud. The balloon was drifting away, with Bluebelle inside the basket waving and shouting. Cloud Cuckoo knew something was wrong. "That's one of the Valley Folk in Professor Clatterpop's balloon," he thought. "I'd better tell someone. But who? The Professor or her friends?"

TELL HER FRIENDS 16

TELL THE PROFESSOR 14

The Professor was busy inventing in his workshop, when Cloud Cuckoo dropped in through the open window. Crash!

"Sorry, Professor," puffed Cloud Cuckoo. "But your balloon has run away with one of the Valley Folk!"

"I'd better set off at once," the Professor declared. "I'll take the walking machine because it will be faster."

The Valley Folk were picnicking when the Professor chugged and rattled into view in his new walking machine. As soon as he told them about Bluebelle, they quickly jumped aboard.

14

"There she is!" shouted Merry, spotting the balloon in the distance. "Let's go that way!" And off they went.

Soon they came to a wide, deep river. "We'll have to find a shallow place to cross," sighed the Professor.

"But the balloon's blowing away over the mountains," said Merry. "Robin and I can look for a quicker way on foot."

GO ON FOOT   26

FOLLOW
THE RIVER   30

Cloud Cuckoo flew over the forest and dived down toward the clearing where Bluebelle's friends were having a picnic. They looked up in fright as the large bird swooped down through the trees. Robin crawled into a hollow log to hide! But Cloud Cuckoo saw his behind sticking out and tapped it with his beak.

"Who . . . Who's there?" whispered Robin.

"Me," said Cloud Cuckoo.

"Who's me?" quivered Robin.

"Well, I don't know who *you* are, but I'm Cloud Cuckoo," said the bird indignantly. "I've come to tell you about one of your friends. She's trapped on a runaway balloon." When they heard the story, Robin, Merry and the others set off right away to find the Professor. If anyone could think of a way to rescue her, he would.

FIND THE PROFESSOR
TURN TO PAGE
18

Professor Clatterpop was in his workshop tinkering with his new walking machine when the Valley Folk arrived. Peeking round the door, all they could see was a pair of feet sticking out from beneath a strange machine that looked like a boat on legs.

"Er . . . Hello, Professor," said Merry.

"Oh, hello, young Merry," said the Professor, sliding out from under the contraption. The Valley Folk clustered around while Merry explained why they were there.

18

"I think we should follow the balloon in the air *and* on the ground," the Professor said at last. "I'll go with some of you in my new walking machine. It will be quicker if we follow the river. Robin, why don't you take someone and set off in my other balloon."

"I'll come with you, Robin," cried Merry eagerly.

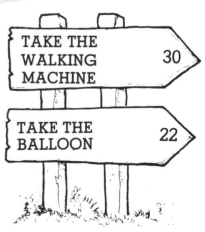

TAKE THE WALKING MACHINE 30

TAKE THE BALLOON 22

19

Cloud Cuckoo clicked his beak together and began to whistle a strange little tune. The sky grew darker and the wind began to blow harder. "Oh dearie me," said Cloud Cuckoo nervously. "I think that might have been the wrong tune." Soon they were both clinging to the basket as it was blown and thrown around the stormy sky.

"Look! What's that?" shouted Bluebelle above the noise. "I thought I saw another balloon!" But when Cloud Cuckoo looked, all he could see were black storm clouds.

"I'm frightened," whimpered Bluebelle, as the ropes strained and creaked in the wind.

"I don't think the storm can last much longer," Cloud Cuckoo said, "but I'll try to carry you down on my back, if you like."

Bluebelle looked at Cloud Cuckoo, who wasn't much bigger than she was. "Oh I don't know. What if I'm too heavy?"

SHE STAYS   24

SHE GOES WITH CLOUD CUCKOO   42

Merry and Robin were just a bit nervous as they set off. They had never been in a balloon before and they felt that it was a long way down to the ground. After a little while, Merry tugged at Robin's sleeve. "Look!" he cried excitedly. "I can see the others in the walking machine."

"And I can see Bluebelle's balloon," shouted Robin. Up ahead, Bluebelle was waving frantically to them. Robin and Merry waved back.

They seemed to be slowly catching up to her when the sky grew darker and streams of gray clouds began to close in. "I've lost sight of her, and it's getting very stormy," cried Robin. "Perhaps we should try to land. I can see a path below us."

"Good idea," answered Merry. "But Bluebelle's balloon might get too far ahead."

THEY KEEP GOING 24

THEY LAND 26

23

There were two balloons hidden in the dark storm clouds. Bluebelle was in one, and her friends Robin and Merry were chasing her in the other. The wind blew the balloons this way and that way and up and down, and then, it blew them both together. Crash!

"Robin! Look! We've found Bluebelle!" cried Merry, as

Bluebelle's frightened face appeared over the side of her basket.

"Hold on tight!" Merry shouted to her. "The balloons are tangled up and yours has got a big tear in it."

Sure enough, the air was escaping from Bluebelle's balloon and it was dragging them all slowly downward.

THE BALLOON
GOES DOWN
TURN TO PAGE
36

25

Robin and Merry found themselves on a path that wound up through the mountains. The two friends set off eagerly, but the path soon became very steep and hard to climb. Then suddenly Robin slipped! Merry grabbed his sleeve, but he slipped too. Down they both fell right into a cold mountain stream.

"Er . . . Robin," whispered Merry. "I don't think we're alone."

There on the bank stood a row of froglike creatures with long legs and round tummies.

"Hello . . . urp, urp," they chorused. "We're the Hoppity-Skips. Are you . . . urp, urp . . . looking for your friends?"

"Are they nearby?" asked Robin hopefully, feeling a little shaky. The Hoppity-Skips all nodded at once.

"I think we should try climbing the mountain again," said Merry. "We'd be able to see Bluebelle's balloon from the top."

THEY JOIN
THEIR   32
FRIENDS

THEY CLIMB
THE   42
MOUNTAINS

They tiptoed quietly toward the rocks. A large shadow flapped and danced across the sand from the other side.

"I don't know what it can be, but it's very big," whispered the Professor. Merry edged round the rocks.

"Ssh," he hissed. "I can hear Bluebelle. We must save her!" They all counted to three, then they charged—straight into the empty, billowing folds of Professor Clatterpop's balloon!

There was Bluebelle, laughing at them, stirring a pot of soup over a little campfire. Next to her sat a large person dressed all in

sacks. The Valley Folk were amazed. "Come and meet the Sandbagger," said Bluebelle. "He lives on the beach in a house made of sandbags. Do you want some soup?"

They were so glad to find Bluebelle safe and sound that they forgot to be annoyed with her for playing in the Professor's balloon, especially when the Sandbagger invited them all to stay for a picnic.

THE PICNIC 44

29

The little group followed the river for quite a while in the walking machine. They were all singing and swaying from side to side with the tune. But they swayed so much that the walking machine began to rock.

"Careful!" shouted the Professor. But it was too late. Slowly the machine toppled over—right into the river! Before the Valley Folk knew if they were upside down or the right side up, they found themselves being hauled to safety by strange, froglike creatures.

"We're the Hoppity-Skips," they said in unison. "We've seen . . . urp, urp . . . two other Valley Folk today. Should we take you to them?" All the Valley Folk thought that was a very good idea.

"I don't know," said the Professor. "We could build a splendid raft out of what's left of the walking machine and sail after Bluebelle."

THEY FOLLOW THE HOPPITY-SKIPS 32

THEY BUILD A RAFT 38

When all the friends met up again, they thanked the Hoppity-Skips and wondered what to do next. "I can't see the balloon now," said Merry. "The last time we saw it, it was heading in that direction." He pointed up a steep hillside. "It's a pity we lost the walking machine," he sighed. "Now we have to go on foot."

It seemed like hours passed before they reached the top. Then Robin cried, "I can see the sea!" and suddenly everyone was scrambling down the cliffs to the beach, laughing and shouting.

"But where's Bluebelle?" said Merry. Everybody fell silent.

Nowhere in the blue skies or blue sea could a balloon be seen. "She *must* have landed on the beach," said Merry, looking around.

"I can smell something cooking," said the Professor, surprised. "It's coming from behind those rocks. Let's take a look."

"Look at this," said Robin, pointing to a strange trail in the sand. "Something very big passed by here. It looks like a monster!"

LOOK BEHIND THE ROCKS   28 ▷

FOLLOW THE MONSTER TRAIL   34 ▷

They followed the trail along the beach. It led to a very odd house made entirely out of bags of sand. "Is anybody there?" called the Professor. A large, friendly round face poked out of a window, so suddenly it made them all jump.

"Hello, I'm the Sandbagger. Who are you?" They told him. And then they told him about Bluebelle.

"I think I know where your little friend is," laughed the Sandbagger. "I've seen the balloon. I'll take you to it."

As they marched along, the Sandbagger told them how he got his name. "You see," he said, "my house is made of sand, and

whenever it rains it starts to fall down. So I make new sandbags to build it up again."

"So that's what made the trail—a sandbag being dragged across the beach!" exclaimed the Professor.

Robin asked the Sandbagger why he didn't live somewhere else. "I'm too big and heavy to climb the cliffs," answered the Sandbagger sadly.

"Look!" cried Merry. "It's the balloon!"

GO TO THE BALLOON
TURN TO PAGE
46

35

They sank down through the clouds. "We're going to come down on the beach, by the sea!" cried Robin.

The balloons landed with a bump, spilling the three of them onto the sand. The yellow and blue balloon shook itself free and drifted out to sea. "Oh dear," said Robin. "What will the Prof . . ."

"Shhh! There's someone else here," whispered Bluebelle.

"Where did you come from, little ones?" boomed a deep, friendly voice. Up marched the Sandbagger, a large, rambling

person with a sandbag tucked under one arm. "I've seen some others like you on the beach today," he told them. "Come with me and I'll show you where they are."

"Yes, please. It must be the Professor and the others," said Robin excitedly.

"Come along then," laughed the Sandbagger. "See if you can keep up!"

FOLLOW
THE SANDBAGGER
TURN TO PAGE
40

37

With the help of the Hoppity-Skips the raft was soon finished.
"All aboard!" called the Professor. Waving good-bye to the
Hoppity-Skips, they set off once again. Soon the river widened,
and the Valley Folk could see seagulls circling above them.

"Look!" cried the Professor. "The sea! And there's Robin and
Merry." They paddled to the beach and jumped out to greet their
friends.

Together again, the little band began searching the beach. They
still hadn't found poor Bluebelle. They came to a huge pile of
rocks. Something large and mysterious was moving behind it.

"I think it's a monster," whispered Robin.
The Professor had spotted footprints in the
sand, beside a strange trail that led up the
beach.

"Someone else must have been here," he
muttered. "Whoever it is might know where
Bluebelle is."

"Or," said Merry nervously, "the monster
could have captured her."

"Well, what should we do?" asked Robin.

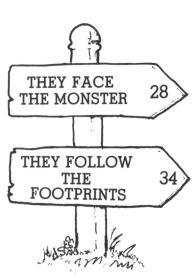

THEY FACE
THE MONSTER   28

THEY FOLLOW
THE
FOOTPRINTS   34

It was hard work following the Sandbagger. He took such big steps! "What a lovely place for a picnic," puffed Merry, wishing they could stop for a rest. Just then, the Sandbagger stopped.

"Here they are," he boomed. How glad they all were to be together again! The Sandbagger laughed to see them so happy.

They soon decided that the Professor should mend the balloon, and that he would fly home and bring everyone back for a picnic by the sea. The Sandbagger looked sad. "I'll be lonely when you

go," he said. "I'm too big and heavy to climb the cliffs. That's why I have to live here, in a house of sand."

"You can come in the balloon, too, and see our village," said Bluebelle kindly. "And if you like it, we'll build you a house there. After the picnic, of course!"

MEND THE BALLOON
TURN TO PAGE
44

41

Robin and Merry had been tramping along for hours, searching everywhere for Bluebelle and the balloon.

"I hope Bluebelle is all right," said Robin. Suddenly, out of the sky, a large, scruffy bird landed in front of them with a thump. Bluebelle tumbled off its back. She stared in amazement at her friends. Then she laughed, and hugged them both.

"Meet Cloud Cuckoo," she gasped. "He rescued me."

"Er . . . it was nothing," said Cloud Cuckoo, embarrassed. And with that he flapped clumsily away.

"Now," said Merry, "all we have to do is find the Professor and

all the others who are looking for you."

To their surprise, they soon saw the seashore ahead. They decided to explore the beach, and were just walking round a huge rock when they came face to face with a giant!

"Looking for your friends, are you?" asked the giant. "This way then. Oh, I'm the Sandbagger, and this is where I live."

FOLLOW
THE SANDBAGGER
TURN TO PAGE
40

43

While the Professor worked on repairing the torn balloon, the Sandbagger took the others to all his favorite places. He showed them rock pools with anemones and crabs, and cool caves glittering with precious stones.

At last the balloon was ready. The Professor waved good-bye as he set off.

After several trips, backward and foward, the whole village of Meadowfree was on the beach.

What a time they had, building sandcastles, diving into the waves, and cooking over an open fire.

When it was time to go home, most of the Valley Folk slept all through the balloon ride. But the Sandbagger, of course, stayed wide awake—he was so excited at the thought of living in a new house all made of wood among his new friends.

As for Bluebelle? "I think," she said to Merry, "in the future I will keep my feet firmly on the ground!"

THE END

They found Bluebelle sitting sadly on the collapsed balloon. She jumped for joy when her friends ran up to her. Professor Clatterpop examined the balloon and said that he could mend it. A few hours later it was ready and they all climbed aboard.

When they reached Meadowfree the Sandbagger was so excited that he ran straight into the forest to choose where he wanted to live. The next day, the whole village helped to build his new wooden home, and when it was finished they had a wonderful party to celebrate.

THE END